Kids vs. Nature

Book 3

Surviving
Horse Island

Written by:
Karl Steam

Illustrated by:
Joshua Lagman

© 2018 Libro Studio LLC

All rights reserved. No part of this publication may be reproduced or transmitted in any form or by any means, electronic or mechanical, including photocopying, recording, or any other information storage and retrieval system, without the written permission of the publisher.

ISBN: 978-1-63578-010-9

Current contact information for Libro Studio LLC can be found at www.LibroStudioLLC.com

Contents

1. The Time Comes — 1
2. Sand — 5
3. The Ocean — 10
4. A Day at the Beach — 13
5. Claws — 16
6. The Herd — 22
7. Don't Worry — 25
8. Gossip — 27
9. Burr — 30
10. A Promise — 34
11. Morning — 39
12. Nice Refreshing Swamp Water — 42
13. Analyzing Image — 48
14. Finally — 52

Surviving
Horse Island

Chapter 1
The Time Comes

Last time, we weren't expecting it. I mean, who'd guess the App could send us on a mission without anyone clicking on it? This time was different though. We knew the App had found its way onto Katie's new phone. There was no doubt in my mind another mission was coming.

I kept checking the time. Not because I wanted class to be over, well that too; but because I wanted to see exactly when the App was sending us on our missions. At 9:42 am, Mrs. Emmons noticed I was staring at the clock.

"Josh. Can you please remind us how to calculate density?"

She knew that I didn't know the answer. That's why she called on me. I hate it when teachers do that. Instead of teaching something interesting, they try to humiliate kids, to scare them enough to pay attention.

And like a sucker, I used to answer questions like these the best I could, hoping I didn't sound like a complete idiot. Then I'd turn red in the face, sit up straight in my chair, like a good little boy, and hope I wouldn't get called on again.

A couple years ago, things changed. I realized that feeling embarrassed and trying harder is the reaction teachers want. It actually encourages more surprise questions in the future. So, I adopted a different approach, one where I don't care if I give a good answer or not. My only goal is to throw the teacher off guard enough to make them think twice before calling on me again.

My favorite thing to do when my name gets called is to look at them funny and say, "That's not my name." I know it only works the first couple days of class, or whenever there's a substitute, but I've been using this trick two years in a row, and believe me, making a teacher stop a lesson to double check the seating chart never gets old.

Usually, teachers take a hint and realize that if they leave me alone, I leave them alone. After that, we get along just fine. Mrs. Emmons is different though. She's a hard teacher to rattle. I tried everything from Pleading the Fifth to completely ignoring her question and asking, "Do you think these pants make my butt look big?" The class even laughed at that last one, which usually frustrates teachers more than anything, but the surprise questions never stopped, and now that it was the end of the school year, I had long since run out of creative ways to answer.

I was about to give her the classic, "I don't know." Which isn't a bad response, but I prefer something a little more original. Luckily, I didn't have time to answer. The beam of light appeared, and I was forced to close my eyes.

Chapter 2
Sand

When I opened my eyes, we were sitting in a circle again. Katie's cell phone was lying on the sand. She reached forward and picked it up.

"You guys, I didn't even bring it to school today. I swear. I thought that maybe if it were far away, it wouldn't be able to send us anywhere."

"Well, it was worth a try," I said.

Tyler stood. "Is this another desert?" he asked.

"I don't know," Melisa said.

Other than a few areas of grass and bushes, we were surrounded by sand.

"There're no cactuses," I pointed out.

"It doesn't matter, not all deserts have *cacti*," Melisa said.

"But it's hot," Tyler said.

"That doesn't matter either. Deserts can be hot or cold. What matters is how little precipitation falls in the area."

I noticed Katie rubbing her stomach. She lifted the front of her shirt. There was a swimming suit underneath. It was all black, except for the App's logo printed across the front.

"What the heck," Katie said.

Melisa had one under her shirt too. I held my pants away from my body and tried to see what was underneath. My underwear was gone. In its place was a set of swimming trunks.

"What are we supposed to do with these?" Katie asked.

"You tell us," Melisa said. "You're the one with the phone."

Katie looked at her phone and tapped the screen. The rest of us moved closer so we could see too.

The last two times we had been transported to the wilderness, the app gave us a mission to complete before we could return home. The first time we had to take a picture of a moose. The second time we had to climb a mountain and take a picture from the top. I was afraid to see what the mission would be this time.

7

"Well, that doesn't help much," Katie said.

I walked to the backpack which was lying nearby. As I came closer, I could see that the canteens were next to it as well.

I looked in the bag. "Just the usual," I told the others, "ropes, a pot, knife, and matches."

After that, we stood there a while. I don't think anyone knew what to do next. At least, I didn't know where to start.

"We can climb that hill and get a better idea of where we are," Melisa finally said.

She walked over to me and picked up one of the canteens before leading the way to a sand dune. It wasn't a tall, steep sand dune like I had seen in pictures before. It was basically a hill, like Melisa said, except it seemed to be a really long, curvy hill that stretched away from us in two directions.

Our feet sunk into the sand each time we took a step, making it a slow and tiring walk to the dune top. Since I was the one who had looked in the backpack, I was stuck carrying it. So, I decided that next time I would let someone else find it.

I was sweating. We all were. The air was different than when we had climbed the mountain in our last mission. It felt humid out today.

We were all breathing hard when Melisa stopped near the top of the hill. She turned. For some reason, she was smiling.

"You're not going to believe this," she said.

By the time we caught up to Melisa, we could see over the top of the hill too. Instead of there being more sand, bushes, and grass like I was expecting, there was water—lots and lots of water.

Chapter 3
The Ocean

Waves crashed against the distant beach. The shore stretched as far as I could see in both directions. Everything beyond the shoreline was blue; blue water, stretching out toward the horizon, where it ran into the blue sky.

Nobody said a thing. I think we were all too surprised to know what to say. We just started walking down the hill. Suddenly, I didn't feel so tired anymore. Everyone else must have felt the same way because we were walking faster and faster. Just after Melisa started jogging, Katie began to sprint. That's when I realized we were racing to the water.

At first, the girls were faster than me and Tyler. I couldn't run very well with the backpack, so I let it slip from my shoulders to the sand. Soon, I passed Tyler. The sound of the waves grew louder. Shirts, pants, shoes, and canteens were dropped as we ran. We had everything off but our swimsuits by the time we leapt into the waves.

Since the girls were ahead of me, they had stopped running through the ocean and were swimming on the surface. I splashed and ran as fast as I could toward them. That's when I noticed one of the waves rising. Within a few seconds, the top turned white, and it tumbled on top of me.

Growing up in Ohio, I had never seen waves like this before, and I definitely never felt them. It turns out that having a wave crash on you feels like a body slam from a pro wrestler. It was sort of like doing a belly flop, except the pain was felt everywhere instead of just my belly. The air was knocked out of my lungs, and I tumbled under the water for a while. Since I didn't know which way was up and which was down, I decided to just wait until the water stopped spinning. Then I figured I would be able to feel which direction my body was floating and know that was the way to the surface.

Instead, my head slammed against the sandy sea bottom. I sat up and realized that I had been washed back to shore. I was expecting to hear the others laughing and making fun of how silly I looked, but nobody seemed to notice. Tyler ran past me. I stood back up and followed him to

Melisa and Katie, who were treading water and bobbing up and down with the ocean. This time, I was more careful about watching for waves that were about to crest.

Chapter 4
A Day at the Beach

We stayed in the water a long time. We splashed, did handstands, and dunked each other. Katie even climbed onto my shoulders and challenged Melisa and Tyler to a chicken fight. Melisa didn't want to chicken fight though. She said she was done swimming and left the water.

When we went back to the beach, we did what I imagined were the normal things people did at the beach. We built castles and took turns burying each other in the sand.

Katie was just starting to collect seashells when Melisa said, "You guys, we should start looking for water."

Katie held her arm toward the ocean. "Ah hello," she said.

"No, I mean drinking water," Melisa clarified.

"Let's wait until later," Katie said. She bent to pick up another shell.

"But it's hot out," Melisa said. "I don't want anyone to get dehydrated again."

Me and Tyler kept pushing driftwood into the sand so that their ends would form a fence around the castle we were making. Katie held a dirty shell in the water so that the waves would wash it clean.

"Come on you guys," Melisa said. "Josh, you'll help me look for water. Won't you?"

"What's wrong with this water?" I asked.

Melisa put her hands on her hips.

"You can't drink ocean water," Tyler said.

"Why not?" I asked.

Tyler shrugged. "I don't know. I think the salt is bad for you."

"Anyone who's done a little research about surviving should know that," Melisa said, "and people can only live a couple days without water, which is why we should start looking for some we can actually drink."

"Relax, will you," Katie said. "We haven't been here that long. Let's have fun for a little while."

Melisa stared at me and Tyler for a few seconds. I think she was waiting for us to say something, but we didn't.

"Fine," she said. "I guess I'm the only responsible person around here."

Melisa turned and collected the canteens that we had scattered along the beach. She walked back up the hill but stopped when she realized nobody was going to follow her. She crossed her arms again, sat on the sand, and waited for us to finish playing.

Chapter 5
Claws

"Hey look," Katie called. She was leaning over and staring at something. At first, I thought that she was looking at another shell, but then she let out a shriek and jumped backward. Whatever it was Katie was looking at, it was moving.

That made me and Tyler stand up in a hurry, and we ran across the beach. As we came closer, something in front of Katie scurried away from us. It was a crab.

The crab was a pale, tan color except for its claws and parts of its legs, which were blue. Most of the time, it just sat in one place and waved its claws in the air when we came too close.

"Blue Crab," the App said after Katie took a picture of it.

"Think we can eat it?" Tyler asked.

His question surprised me. Food definitely wasn't the first thing I thought of when I saw the crab. I mean, it basically looked like a giant sideways-walking spider. Yummy, right?

Katie stroked her chin and read the App's description of the crab. "I mean, it doesn't say, but I don't know why not," she said, "as long as we cook it."

"Do you know how to cook a crab?" I asked.

"I think you boil them," Katie said. "Just like lobster."

Katie seemed to know what she was talking about, so she and Tyler began to gather the driftwood that lined the beach. I was in charge of keeping an eye on the crab. Eventually, Tyler went to get the matches from the backpack, which was still where I had dropped it during our footrace.

"I bet you wish we had found some water now," Melisa said. She had been avoiding us for quite a while, but now walked closer.

"We're going to use ocean water," Katie said. "We won't drink it, just use it for boiling. The salt in the water might actually make it taste better. Natural seasoning."

I wasn't sure if Melisa would like the idea of cooking with ocean water, but she didn't argue. She sat next to the fire and waited while Tyler scooped ocean water into the pot.

"We're ready," Katie called when the water began to boil.

I used sticks to pinch the crab's shell and pick it up, then slowly walked it to the pot and set it in.

"Gross," Melisa said.

I have to say, I'm not fond of cooking live animals, but Katie said that's how real chefs do it. The crab's tan and blue colors disappeared, and its body turned a deep red color, even the claws. It was looking more and more like food.

After a while, we pulled the crab back out with the sticks and let it cool off. Tyler cracked a leg open, exposing the steamy meat inside. He blew on it. Then he took a bite.

"It's good, like the ones at that Chinese restaurant on fifth avenue.

After that, we all tried a piece. Tyler was right. It was good. The problem was, between the four of us, the little crab didn't even come close to filling us up. So we searched for more crabs. Even Melisa left the fire to help look.

It took twenty minutes, but we eventually found five more crabs and carried them to the pot too. Since we could only fit two in at a time, it was a full-time job making sure the others didn't run too far away. We constantly tried to scare them back to the fire and sometimes had to carry them back with the sticks.

After we had eaten two more and had another two cooking, there was only one left to babysit. That gave us a little time to relax.

19

I leaned back in the sand and watched little birds with long skinny legs run by the water. Whenever a wave washed on shore, the birds ran just far enough on land so that only their legs got wet. Then they followed the water as it got sucked back into the ocean. They used their beaks to pick things out of the wet sand to eat before the next wave came.

I liked these birds, so I had Katie take a picture of one. The App called them sandpipers. For some reason, watching them run with the waves made everything feel peaceful. The ocean was more beautiful than I had ever imagined.

While I was admiring the view, I happened to glance further down the beach. In the distance, I noticed something else running. They were horses.

Chapter 6
The Herd

I stood and pointed. "You guys. Look."

The horses looked tiny in the distance. A whole herd was running onto the beach, maybe twenty or twenty-five total. They galloped right into the ocean too. Most stood there, letting the waves crash against their bodies. A few splashed and chased each other through the shallows.

Melisa jogged closer. "Let's go," she said.

The rest of us followed. It took a few minutes to get close enough for a better view.

"Do you think we can ride them?" Tyler asked.

"I wouldn't," Melisa said. "They might be wild."

"They don't look that wild to me," Tyler said.

The horses saw us and trotted away from the ocean, so Melisa slowed to a walk. "I think we're close enough," she said. "Take a picture."

Katie held up her phone, then lowered it.

"What are you doing?" Melisa asked.

"I don't want to leave. Can't we stay a while?"

"No," Melisa said, "we need to get back home."

"But I want to find more shells," Katie said.

Melisa put her hands on her hips. "What's the point? It's not like you can bring them back with us."

Katie shrugged. "I still like finding them."

Melisa glanced at the herd. They were traveling up the hill. "You don't get to decide what we do just because it's your phone," she said.

"Fine, let's vote then," Katie said. She raised her hand. "Who wants to stay a little longer?"

The girls looked at me and Tyler. I looked at the horses, then at the ocean.

"When's the next time you'll be by an ocean?" Katie asked.

Tyler slowly lifted his arm. "I'll stay."

"Come on you guys," Melisa pleaded.

The herd reached the top of the hill, and the leaders were disappearing over the crest.

I avoided eye contact but could tell Melisa was staring at me. "We might as well stay a little while," I finally said. "We have food to eat, and it doesn't seem like a very dangerous place."

Melisa watched the last horse trot out of sight. As soon as it did she turned to us. "I hate you guys," she said, then crossed her arms over her stomach and stomped back to the fire.

Chapter 7
Don't Worry

Melisa yanked the backpack from the sand.

"What are you doing?" Katie asked.

"A fourth of the matches are mine," Melisa said. "I'm taking them with me... and some of the rope too." She opened the pocket knife and cut a section of the rope off for herself.

"Where are you going?" Tyler asked.

"Far away."

"Just wait a minute," I said.

"No, you guys stay here and enjoy your vacation. I'll take care of myself." Melisa dropped a few matches into her empty canteen and closed the lid. "Besides, this *'doesn't seem like a very dangerous place,'*" she said, mocking my voice. "So, don't worry about me."

Melisa wrapped her rope into a coil, put the canteen over her shoulder, and walked away from us again. This time, she was heading for the hill.

Katie rolled her eyes. "Let her go if she wants to."

"You should take some crab with you," Tyler shouted. He held a couple uneaten legs in the air.

"I'll get my own," Melisa shouted back. A little while later, she disappeared over the top of the hill, just as the horses had.

"She'll be back," Katie said.

I didn't say anything, but I didn't expect Melisa to come back. I figured she'd be too stubborn, even if she wanted to. Besides, something like this had happened before, when we had gotten lost picking berries. Melisa didn't come back that time either.

Chapter 8
Gossip

Katie seemed to be the only one having fun after that. She had us collect a big pile of driftwood so that we could have a large campfire in the evening. Then she made three piles of sand around the fire so that we could rest our backs against them, sort of like we were sitting in La-Z-Boy recliners. Katie even dug little depressions for our butts and slightly elevated our feet.

I'll admit, the chairs were comfy, but I didn't feel like relaxing.

"This is going to be great," Katie kept saying. "The sun will set over the water, and we'll watch the stars come out again. Then we'll fall asleep, listening to the sound of crashing waves."

All I can say is that things didn't exactly happen like Katie planned. The sun didn't set over the water. It sank lower in the sky behind us and eventually disappeared behind the hill. Then the sky turned dark blue as the daylight dimmed.

"That's alright," Katie said. "We'll just watch the sun rise over the ocean tomorrow."

"I'm getting thirsty," Tyler said after we finished having another meal of crab.

"It's going to be dark soon," Katie said. "Just hold off until morning."

Tyler didn't argue. He poked the coals with a

stick. His eyes looked droopy, and he yawned.

"We should have listened to her," I said. "You were dehydrated during the last mission," I told Tyler. "We should have looked for water right away this time. Melisa was right."

"That's cute," Katie said. "Too bad you didn't say that earlier. She would've wanted to hear that."

"Why would you call that cute?" I asked.

"No reason," Katie said, but she pretended to turn her face away from me so that I couldn't see her smiling. "It's nothing," she added.

Seriously, I thought Katie was being weird, so I tried to ignore her. Some people get that way when they're tired. Take my friend Mark for example.

Whenever we have a sleepover, and he stays up late, he gets kind of hyper and starts to do stupid stuff. It's like he's overtired and suddenly thinks everything is funny and says a bunch of goofy things. I figured Katie might be like that, and would probably crash in fifteen minutes.

"You know she likes you right?" Katie said.

"Who? Melisa?" I asked. "No, she doesn't."

Katie shrugged. "I know. Like I said, 'it's nothing.'"

"Why would you think that?" I asked.

Katie leaned forward in her sand chair. It was like she had been waiting for me to ask, and finally had an excuse to gossip.

"Well for starters, she left the water as soon as I climbed on your shoulders for a chicken fight."

"Big deal," I said.

"I know, that's what I thought, until later, when she asked you in particular if you'd help her look for drinking water. Then I started to wonder if maybe she was a little jealous that you were going to be on my team for the chicken fight."

"Maybe that's why she handed her glasses to you instead of me to light the fire during our first mission," Tyler said.

"And don't forget that you tried to rescue her from the snake in the last mission," Katie added.

I shook my head. "I think you're imagining things."

"Maybe I'm wrong," Katie said. She folded her hands behind her head, leaned back in her sand recliner and stared at the stars. "I just thought I felt a vibe."

Chapter 9
Burr

I woke up in the middle of the night with goosebumps on my arms and legs. The air was cool, and a breeze blew most of the fire's heat toward the ocean. Even though the waves were moving against the wind, they seemed to be washing further up the beach than they had earlier in the evening.

I tried finding a comfortable spot by the fire. It was difficult. Katie and Tyler were sleeping in the best spots. They were close enough to be warm, and on the side that the wind was coming from. The only warm places left for me to lie were downwind from the fire, which meant I'd have smoke and sparks blowing on me. I really wished I had something warmer than my t-shirt. Couldn't the App at least pack us some sleeping bags?

A flicker caught my eye. There was an orange glow far down the beach, probably Melisa's fire. I remembered how scary spending the night in the forest had been. Although I didn't expect to hear a wolf howl or see a raccoon steal someone's sock, I figured even the beach might seem scary at night, especially if you're alone.

I was having a hard time sleeping anyway, so I decided to check on Melisa. I walked by the ocean since my feet didn't sink down as far in the wet, firm sand. A full moon had appeared sometime during the night. It was huge, yellow, and hung low enough in the horizon for its reflection to glitter across the waves. The longer I walked, the higher it rose in the sky. Eventually, it was just a small white circle.

Melisa's fire was mostly coals when I arrived. There was a lot of driftwood on this section of the beach too, more than I had seen anywhere else. She had made some sort of shelter out of the longer pieces. A neatly stacked pile of firewood was nearby.

Moonlight passed through the gaps and holes of her shelter. I could see Melisa resting. Her glasses lay on the sand beside her. Slow, gentle breaths made her look relaxed, even peaceful, but glistening tear streaks proved otherwise. She had probably cried herself to sleep.

Chapter 10
A Promise

I set some wood on the coals. Sparks swirled into the air.

Melisa flinched.

"It's just me," I said. "Didn't mean to wake you. I just wanted to warm up before going back."

Melisa leaned on her elbow. "What are you doing here?"

"I don't know... I saw your fire and wanted to see how you were doing."

"Well, I'm fine."

"I see that." I held my hands over the fire and stood as close to it as I could.

Melisa moved to the side of her shelter and sat cross-legged. "It's warm in here," she said, then took a sip from her canteen.

I crawled in and sat beside her. She was right. It was warm inside. The driftwood helped to block the breeze and trapped some of the fire's heat.

"Looks like you found water," I said.

"No thanks to you."

I wanted to say sorry for not helping but didn't. I've never been great at apologizing to people. It makes me feel uncomfortable.

"I know... We should have helped," I finally said.

Melisa swallowed hard, which made me wonder if she had a lump in her throat.

"It's not just the water," she said. "I almost died during the last mission, and it's like nobody even cares. All I want to do is go home, but the only thing you guys are worried about is playing."

"We care," I said.

"No, you don't," she said. "I asked you to research ways to survive before this mission, and you didn't even do that. You might think this App is just a big game, but I'm really scared right now."

Melisa's voice was shaking, making it sound like she was about to cry again.

"I tried researching, but not for very long," I admitted. "Most of the websites I went to talked about bringing along extra things like food, water, matches, and clothes before you go hiking. Stuff like that doesn't help us though."

"I know what you mean," Melisa said. "They say that most of the time the best thing to do when you're lost in the wild is to stay where you are, that way you don't get more lost."

"Then blow a whistle and make smoke signals until a rescue team can find you," I added.

Melisa yawned and laid down. "Exactly. The problem is, we're on our own. We don't have anyone to call for help." After a pause, she lifted her canteen. "You want some?"

"Sure," I said, trying not to sound too desperate, even though my mouth felt as dry as the sand.

"What do you think would've happened if I had died from that snake bite before we finished the mission?" Melisa asked. "Would I have reappeared in the classroom, somehow back to normal? Or do you think once we die, we're gone forever? Like if our body would reappear when the mission is over, but we just drop-dead right away."

I handed the canteen back and laid down too. "I don't know," I said, "but I don't want to find out."

"Me either," Melisa said.

I folded my arms across my chest and closed my eyes.

"Josh?"

"Yea."

"Promise me something?"

"What?"

"If something happens to me, will you tell my parents I love them?"

"Don't talk like that," I said. "We're gonna be alright."

"Do you promise?" Melisa said.

I wasn't sure if she was asking again whether I would tell her parents she loves them or if she wanted me to promise her that we would be alright. I figured it didn't really matter though. My answer was the same either way.

"Yea, I promise."

After I said those words, something inside of me felt a little different. From that point on, I knew it didn't matter what missions the App decided to give us. I only had one real mission now. My mission was to stay alive and to make sure that everyone else did too.

Chapter 11
Morning

"Well, aren't you two adorable."

I recognized Katie's voice and slowly opened my eyes. It was light outside, even though it was cloudy. A thin wisp of smoke rose from a pile of ashes. That's all that was left of the fire.

I sat up.

"Why did you ditch us?" Tyler asked. "We thought you drowned."

"I didn't ditch you."

"You left and didn't tell us where you were going," Tyler said.

"You guys were hogging the warm spots around the fire, so I decided to..." I couldn't even finish my thought. "Why are you all wet?" I asked.

"Because someone left without telling us that the ocean was rising," Katie said.

Melisa smiled, then crawled out of the shelter. "You guys slept below the tide line?"

"Apparently," Katie said. "We had a wave wash into us while we were sleeping."

"Yea, when it hit our fire, it made a loud POOF sound. Then the coals started hissing and steaming," Tyler added. "I thought a bomb had gone off."

"After the wave was sucked back into the ocean, we noticed you were gone," Katie explained. "We thought it pulled you in while you slept."

"Sorry, I didn't think it would be such a big deal," I said. "I just couldn't sleep and decided to make sure Melisa was O.K."

"Right," Katie said, except she said it really slow so that I would know she was being sarcastic. "And how was your night?"

"Just shut up Katie," I said.

"You should tell us where you're going next time," Tyler said.

"Don't worry. I will."

"That's the tide line. Right there," Melisa said. She walked to an area in front of the driftwood that had piled up on shore. "You need to make camp above this line to avoid the high tides."

"Well, we know that now," Katie said. "Now, let's go."

"Go where?" Melisa asked.

"Go find the horses," Katie said, but she spoke in a deep voice and raised her eyebrows as if she were also saying "duh."

Melisa put her hands on her hips. "Oh, so now you want to go home?"

"Yea, this place sucks," Katie said. "I'm wet, cold, hungry, thirsty, and it's too cloudy to even see the sunrise."

"Alright, let's go then," Melisa agreed.

Chapter 12
Nice Refreshing Swamp Water

We walked all the way back down the beach to where we saw the horses the day before. Their hoof prints were still in the sand, but we didn't try to track them. The trail was too old.

We made another campfire, cooked a few more crabs, and waited. We waited... and waited... and waited until midafternoon, but we didn't see a single horse.

"Let's get some water," Tyler said, after letting the last drops fall from his canteen and into his mouth.

Melisa was nice enough to share her water with the rest of us, but one canteen split four ways didn't amount to much.

"Let's stay a little longer," Melisa said. "We might miss the horses when they come back."

"We've been here all day," Katie said. "They're not coming back."

"Where else have you seen a horse?" Melisa asked. "Right now, this place is our best bet."

"Maybe Katie's right," I said. "Maybe they aren't coming back."

Melisa crossed her arms and looked at me.

"They went in the water yesterday, right?" I asked. "Well, it was also hot and sunny out yesterday. They probably wanted to cool off. But now that it's cold out..."

"They won't have a reason to come to the beach," Melisa finished.

"Exactly."

Melisa scanned the shoreline one last time to make sure no horses were in sight. "Alright, follow me," she said.

Melisa led us down the beach, over the hill, and to an area that had trees and bushes. Eventually, we came to a wide grassy area that surrounded what looked like a large pond.

"Finally," Katie said.

"Not exactly." Melisa pointed to a dark spot along the edge of the pond. "See, that's where I made a fire yesterday to purify the water, but when I drank some, it was still salty."

"But it's not ocean water. Is it?" I asked.

"I think the ocean water might be mixing with it somehow. I had to walk further inland to find water that didn't taste so salty."

We followed Melisa along the edge of the pond, eventually moving back into a forest. We didn't stop until we were next to a flooded marshy area.

"This is it," she said.

Katie wrinkled her nose. "You got your water from here?" she asked. "I can't believe you gave us swamp water to drink."

Tyler knelt beside the water and unscrewed the lid to his canteen. "Well, don't drink any if you don't want to," he said.

"Josh, I'll fill yours if you get the fire ready," Melisa said.

I was taking the canteen off my shoulder when Katie turned. Her eyes darted toward the trees. "Did you guys hear that?" she asked.

I imagined a moose charging from the trees, then realized I was being ridiculous and shook that thought away. "Hear what?" I asked.

Katie held a finger to her lips. "Shhhh. Listen."

We stayed perfectly still.

"It was a horse," Katie said.

We listened some more.

I took the canteen the rest of the way off my shoulder. "I don't hear anything," I said.

Katie shook her head. "I swear I heard a horse." She walked into the forest.

"Maybe she did hear something," Melisa said, and we tried our best to catch up.

There was a faint nickering.

"Did you hear that one?" Katie asked

"Yea, I heard it," Tyler said.

Melisa quickened her pace. "Me too."

We traveled deeper into the wooded marshland. After a while, it was hard to tell if we were still moving in the right direction. Each time that happened, we stopped to listen. Once we heard another horse call, we knew which way to go again.

We came to a grassy area and another pond. This time, there were horses standing at the edge of the water. It was a herd of about seven or eight. Most of them, eating grass, but a few were drinking.

"They probably come here when they're thirsty," Tyler said. "They know this is fresh water."

Melisa crouched so that the horses wouldn't see her. "Take a picture," she whispered.

The rest of us crouched too. Katie took the phone out, aimed it at the herd, and snapped a photo.

Chapter 13
Analyzing Image

"Analyzing image..." the phone said. "Chincoteague Mare."

"Why isn't it counting down?" Katie asked.

"Try again," I said.

Katie took another picture.

"Analyzing image... Chincoteague Mare," the app said.

"They must not be stallions," Tyler said.

"What does a stallion look like?" Melisa asked.

All the horses lifted their heads from the water, their ears held high. They peered at the forest, listening for something. They didn't move for the longest time, except for the occasional flick of the tail and twitch of the shoulder.

"What are they looking at?" Katie asked.

I shook my head.

Two horses bolted from the trees. Their leg muscles rippled as they ran across the grass. They stopped, panting at a base of a sand dune. They looked tired, but it didn't stop them from rearing onto their hind legs and kicking each other.

"They're fighting," Tyler said.

Katie lifted her phone again. "I'll bet you anything those are stallions."

The electronic click was heard.

"Analyzing Image..."

I held my breath.

"Chincoteague Stallion ... Mission complete, Returning home in one minute..."

The stallions stopped kicking. Their front hoofs slammed to the ground. The brown horse lunged at the one with white and bit its neck. I'm not kidding. It opened its mouth real wide and bit the other horse, the way a dog bites a mailman.

"Returning in 45 seconds..."

"I can't believe he just did that," Melisa said.

The white horse tried to run away but was followed. It kicked its back legs in the air, and a hoof hit the brown horse on the side of the face.

"Ouch, these guys are dirty fighters," Tyler said.

"They definitely seem like wild horses to me," Katie added.

"Returning in 30 seconds..."

Fighting must be a lot of work. Both stallions stood and stared at each other for a while. The sides of their bodies seemed to pulse with each breath.

I glanced at the phone and saw the picture of the firefly. The tail blinked on and off.

"Returning in 15 seconds...," the voice said.

The white horse charged. The brown one rose on its hind legs again and waved its front hooves. The white horse jumped in the air and came crashing into the brown one, which stumbled to the side.

"Returning in 5... 4..."

"Josh. Mass divided by volume," Melisa said.

"3... 2..."

"What?" I asked.

"1..."

The firefly's tail had grown brighter with each blink. Now the whole screen glowed. A pulse of light appeared, forcing my eyes to shut.

Chapter 14
Finally

When my eyes opened, we were in Mrs. Emmons' room.

"Josh," Mrs. Emmons said.

"What?" I looked around the room. Everyone was staring at me.

"Can you please answer the question?"

I blinked a couple times, then looked at Melisa. "Mass divided by volume," I said.

Mrs. Emmons lifted an eyebrow. She nodded. "That's right class, divide the mass by the volume to find density, and remember to label it with units cubed..."

After that, I knew my question was over, and I tuned Mrs. Emmons out again.

A girl named Abby, reached into her pocket, pulled out a phone, and held it under her desk so that Mrs. Emmons wouldn't see.

Abby leaned toward Katie's desk and whispered, "What did you do that for?"

Katie looked confused.

"Why'd you call me?" Abby asked.

"I didn't," Katie said.

"Yea, you did." Abby looked up, making sure Mrs. Emmons was still facing the whiteboard. She turned the phone to prove Katie that she had a missed call from her.

"Sorry, it must have dialed accidentally," Katie said.

I saw Abby's screen before she put it back in her pocket. She did have a missed call from Katie, and it happened at exactly 9:42 am.

👍 Next in the Series

Scenes from Book #3

Would You Have Survived?

Why can't people drink ocean water?

Kidney's filter excess salt from the body, but they need water to do this. Although seawater is mostly made of water, it does not provide enough water for the kidneys to excrete all the salt that it contains. This forces the body to use water it already has to get rid of the extra salt, leaving the body even more dehydrated than it was before.

Couldn't you boil the ocean water first?

Boiling ocean water may kill bacteria but does not remove the salt. The only way boiling seawater will help you get drinking water is if you're able to capture the water vapor that rises.

Why capture water vapor?

Boiling seawater does not remove the salt, but it does cause water to evaporate. If you can capture this water vapor, it will be pure water.

How do you capture water vapor?

If a plastic tarp is held above boiling seawater, the steam will condense on it, and the droplets can be directed into a drinking container.

If you don't have a sheet of plastic, you can use a cloth instead. Drape the cloth above the boiling seawater and allow steam to saturate it. Then you can squeeze water from the cloth—right into your mouth or a drinking container.

"Wild" Horses

Do wild horses really exist?

Sort of, most horses that people consider to be "wild" are actually feral horses. Feral horses are untamed horses that live in the wild, but they have ancestors that had once been domesticated.

Where do feral horses come from?

A feral horse herd usually starts when domesticated horses escape or are released into the wild. As generations pass, these horses become unaccustomed to humans and captivity.

Where do feral horses live?

Feral horses are more common than you might think. They live in many places throughout the world. As of 2018, the U.S Department of the Interior estimates that there are over 60,000 feral horses within the United States. Most of them live in western states, such as Nevada, Wyoming, California, Utah, and Oregon.

Do feral horses really live on Islands?

Some do. The setting of this story was inspired by the horses of Assateague Island, which is a barrier island on the Atlantic coast, not far from Washington DC.

How did horses get to Assateague Island?

Nobody knows for sure, but there are a few legends regarding this mystery. Some say that a Spanish ship sunk near the island, and the horses on board swam to shore and became feral. Others claim that pirates brought horses there. It is also known that early colonial settlers allowed horses and cattle to graze on the island.

Can you ride a feral horse?

Feral horses are not tame and can be very dangerous. The horses of Assateague Island are more accustom to humans than most feral horses but should still not be approached.

How are they dangerous?

They will kick and bite when they are upset. Males will aggressively defend their herds and females are protective of their foals.

Go to www.karlsteam.com/books/surviving-horse-island/ to see a video of some people getting hurt by Assateague Island horses and to learn about the importance of giving them space.

Ways to stay safe around feral horses:
- Horse selfies are tempting, but do not get too close.
- If they approach you, back away.
- Do not feed them or give them water.
- Do not try to scare them away.

Crabs

Why are they called blue crabs?

Because they have blue claws. Its shell is mostly brown though.

Can you really eat them?

Sure, they're considered a delicacy along a great portion of America's Atlantic coastline.

Do you really boil crabs?

A lot of people do. You can also roast them over a fire, grill them, or bakc thcm in an oven.

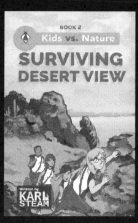
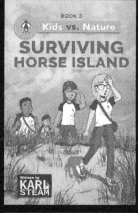

Made in the USA
Coppell, TX
04 November 2019